Produced by Kroha Associates, Inc.
Middletown, Connecticut.

Printed in the United States of America.

ISBN 1-56326-121-9

Treasures
In The Attic

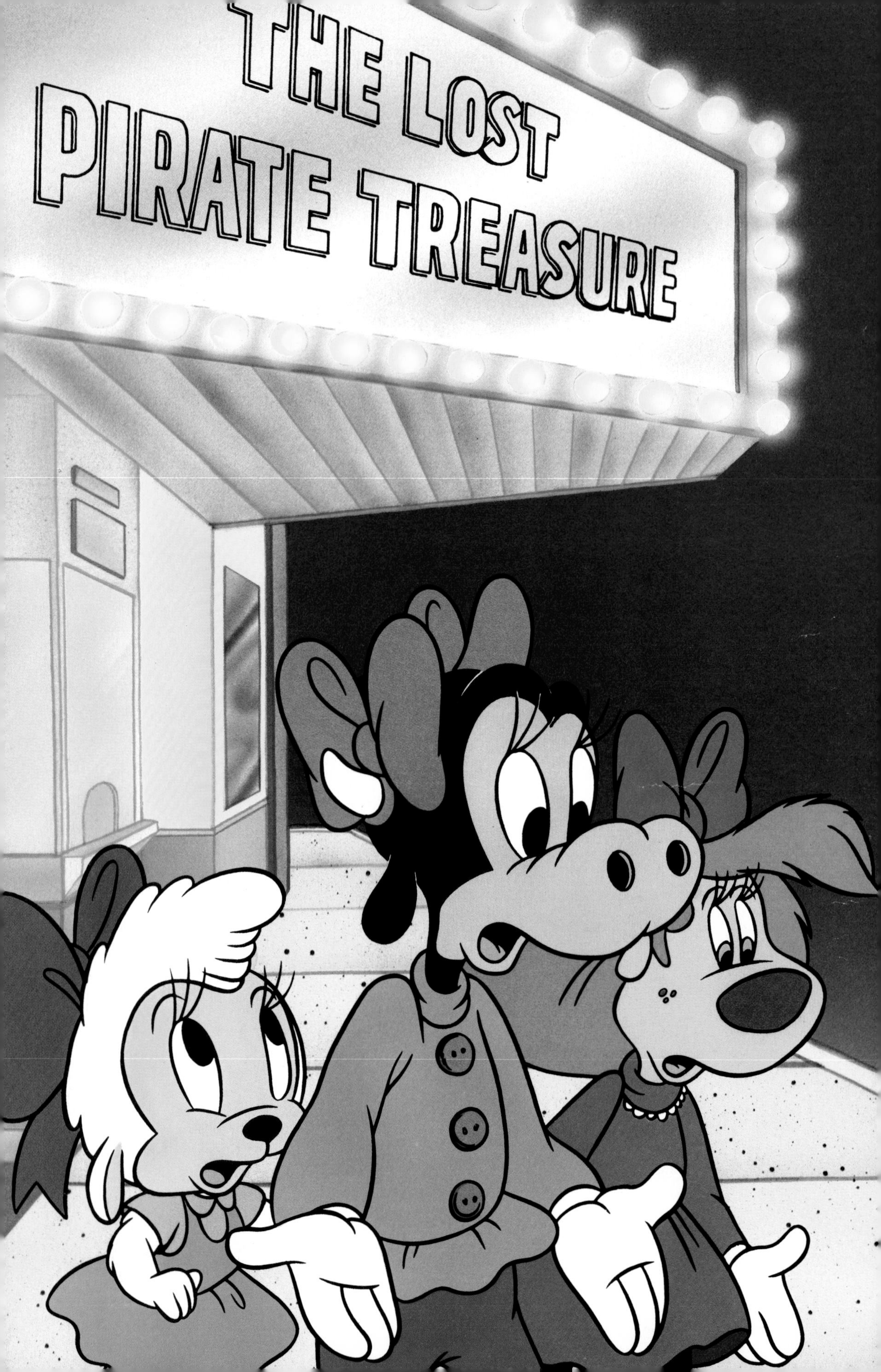
THE LOST
PIRATE TREASURE

One evening, Minnie and her friends went to see a movie about a group of adventurous girls who found a pirate treasure.

"That was the most exciting movie I ever saw!" Daisy exclaimed as everyone left the theater. "I especially liked the part when the girls found the lost treasure!"

"I wish something that great would happen to us," Penny said. "But nothing ever does."

"All we do is play, and go to school, and do our chores and homework," Clarabelle sighed. "Nothing interesting ever happens around here."

"Just think of all the fun we could have if we found a treasure," Penny said. "We'd have enough money to go to every sports event in town."

"Yes," Daisy agreed. "If we discovered a chest filled with gold, we could buy all the beautiful party dresses we wanted."

"I'd throw a party," Clarabelle said. "I'd invite everyone I know and serve huge banana splits with six kinds of toppings."

"Dreaming is okay," Daisy said. "But we'll never find a REAL treasure, and we'll never have an adventure as exciting as the one the girls in the movie had."

The next morning, Minnie was cleaning her room when she had a wonderful idea. *I'm going to surprise my friends with a real adventure!* she thought.

As soon as her room was tidy, Minnie went to work on the surprise for her friends. First, she gathered all her favorite souvenirs of fun times she'd had with Daisy, Penny, Clarabelle, and Lilly. With Fifi trotting happily behind her, Minnie carried the reminders to the attic, put them in a big trunk, locked the lid, and hid the key. Then Minnie got her camera and hid it behind the trunk. Wanting to be part of the fun, Fifi tucked her favorite bone behind the trunk, too! Next, Minnie drew a map, then wrote some funny clues and hid them in her backyard.

When everything was ready, Minnie telephoned her friends. "Come over to my house," she told them. "I've found a map, and I need you to help me look for the treasure! Let's all dress up as pirates — just like the girls in the movie!"

Soon Daisy, Clarabelle, Lilly, and Penny were at Minnie's door wearing scarves and eye patches and big gold earrings. "Where's the map?" Penny asked, waving a little shovel.

"Here it is," Minnie said, as she handed Daisy the map. "Follow the directions on the map, and you'll find the first clue."

"'Go twenty paces out the back door, then turn to the right and walk ten more,'" Daisy read.

"Well, what are we waiting for?" Penny shouted as she ran to the back door. "One, two, three, four...." Penny began walking with Clarabelle, Daisy, and Lilly close behind. When Penny had counted all the steps, she was in the middle of Minnie's vegetable garden. "Now what?" she asked.

"Read the rest of the clue, Daisy," Minnie said, smiling.

"'When you reach the tomatoes red and big, take a shovel and start to dig,'" Daisy read. Penny dug a small hole with her shovel. There was a glass jar in the hole, and inside the jar was a piece of paper.

"It's the next clue!" Clarabelle shouted. "What does it say?"

"'Look around and you will see, the next clue hidden in a tree!'"
Lilly read the clue aloud.

"I know!" Clarabelle shouted. "The clue must be in the hollow of
Minnie's old oak tree!"

The girls ran to the tree and peered inside the hole in its trunk.
Sure enough, the next clue was there. "'A key to more excitement
lies, in the attic near someone's eyes,'" Daisy read.

"What does that mean?" Penny asked, frowning a little.

"I think it means we need to look for a key in the attic," Daisy
explained. "Let's go!"

Minnie smiled as she followed her friends into the house and up the attic stairs.

"I see the key!" Penny shouted. "And it's near someone's eyes, too!" Daisy laughed as she pointed to a painting of Fifi that was leaning against the attic wall. Minnie had taped the key onto the picture, and had placed another note below the key.

" 'For fun and adventure that's the best, take a look in the treasure chest,' " Penny read.

"There it is, in that corner!" Penny yelled, running over to the big, wooden trunk.

"Here, Minnie, it's your trunk. You open it," Daisy said as she gave Minnie the key.

"Oh, no!" Minnie said happily. "I want you to open it!"

Clarabelle, Penny, and Lilly crowded around as Daisy put the key in the lock. "What do you think is in there?" Penny wondered aloud. "Maybe it's a real treasure just like the girls found in the movie!"

"This is the most exciting thing that's ever happened to me," said Lilly.

"Me, too!" Clarabelle exclaimed. "Hurry, Daisy!"

Daisy quickly turned the key, and Minnie's friends all leaned in close to get the first look at what was inside the trunk. But when they looked under the lid, they were very disappointed.

"It's just a bunch of old pictures and papers," Penny moaned, staring into the trunk.

"I don't see anything that looks like a treasure," Clarabelle agreed sadly.

"There's nothing exciting in here," Daisy sighed. "I thought we'd find something really terrific!"

Even Lilly nodded unhappily.

"Wait! You haven't really looked at what's in the trunk yet," Minnie told her friends. She reached in and pulled out a pair of swim goggles.

"Oh, I remember those!" Penny exclaimed. "You always bring them along when we go to the beach, Minnie, so we can take turns looking under the water with them."

"That's right!" Clarabelle chimed in. "Once I even saw a whole school of little silvery fish swimming right beside my toes. I was so surprised!"

"What else is in there?" Penny asked, reaching into the trunk. "Hey, look at this, everyone!" She held up a long red and green paper chain. "Here's a piece of the paper chain we made during the holidays last year!"

"I remember," Daisy said. "It went all through Minnie's house. It was probably the longest paper chain in the world!"

"It was so funny when Fifi got all tangled up in it," Penny said, laughing.

"It sure was!" Clarabelle added, grinning.

Next, Daisy pulled out a red plastic flashlight. She blinked it on and off. "This reminds me of our pajama parties when we make creepy, silly shadow pictures on the walls in the dark!" she said.

"Me, too!" Lilly agreed. "Those shadow pictures always give me the shivers, but they make me laugh, too!"

"Look! My favorite dress-up dress," Lilly exclaimed as she held up a purple dress with sparkly beads down the front. "I love it when we dress up and make up pretend stories about being princesses. It's one of my favorite things to do."

"I like it when we fly kites together," Penny said, holding up a kite. "And the times when we play softball in the park, too!" Clarabelle added. "It's really exciting when our team wins!"

"We make a pretty good team, whatever we do," Lilly said.

"Just looking at all these things makes me remember how many great adventures we've had together," Daisy said thoughtfully. "I guess this is a kind of treasure, after all!"

"It sure is," Minnie said. "Let's all take something to help us remember all the fun we've had."

"That's a wonderful idea, Minnie," Daisy exclaimed. "I'd like the flashlight, and I'll remember to bring it to our next slumber party."

"And I'd like to fly this kite," Penny said.

"You can have the purple dress, Lilly," Minnie offered. "And Clarabelle, you can have the goggles, if you want them."

"Thanks, Minnie," Clarabelle said, grinning as she tried on the goggles. "But if we take these things, what will you have?"

Minnie reached behind the trunk and pulled out her camera. "I'll have a picture of all of you," she said as she pressed the button, "so I can always remember our treasure hunt!"

After her friends helped her put the rest of the things back in the trunk, Minnie closed the lid and put their photograph on the top.

"That was the most exciting treasure hunt ever," Daisy said as everyone headed downstairs, carrying their treasures.

"I'm glad you thought so," Minnie said as she smiled at her friends, "because I think sharing adventures with friends like you is the very best treasure of all!"

Tell me about a "treasure" you have that reminds you of an exciting time with your friends or family. Please use the enclosed letter. I promise to write back soon.